Secrets of a perfect Marriage

Paul Gottman

ISBN:
979-8-8472-4930-0

DEDICATION

This book is dedicated To the love of my lovely mum who has been my source of confidence and encouragement.

CONTENTS

ACKNOWLEDGMENTS

"I have to start by thanking my awesome wife, Michelle. From reading early drafts to giving me advice on the cover to keeping the munchkins out of my hair so I could edit, she was as important to this book getting done as I was. Thank you so much, dear."

INTRODUCTION

How can u tell whether your marriage is doing well or not? this is a query that is really worth researching. particularly, if you have been considering something. its a good idea to physically examine your relationship to see if it meets the criteria for a healthy marriage.

This Book reveals 7 tips to a perfect relationship.

COMMUNICATION

Communication brings lovers together and makes it easy for them to build chemistry and love. The conversations you have with your significant other play a strong role in determining how happy, fun and strong your relationship will be.

No matter how difficult some topics may seem sometimes, discussing them will help ease a lot of tension and leave room for your relationship to grow. You'll also find that you both understand each other better.

The value of communication in marriage is frequently undervalued since many couples believe that their daily banter—or lack thereof—does not significantly affect their lives on a daily basis. However, communication serves as the means through which all other significant aspects of marriage are carried out. If you claim to love someone but don't show it via your words and deeds, you aren't treating your spouse rightly. Tell someone you trust them if you do. Communication should be a priority in marriage.Your marriage has a decent chance of being happy and healthy if you can communicate honestly. In fact, as it establishes the proper foundation for the relationship, communication should be valued from the early stages of courtship.

It doesn't matter whether you are in a new relationship or you've been married for years. These topics will not only help you get closer to your lover; it will also give you ideas on what to talk about when it feels like you are running out of topics. And you can always refine and repeat them as you and your partner will always have different answers each time they come up. This way, you'll never run out of interesting conversations.

Verbal communication

Everyone enjoys hearing compliments on how they appear. Everybody enjoys being told they are loved. Verbal communication is crucial to a successful marriage because it allows you to convey your emotions to your partner through your words. The other person might never really get how much you love them if you don't express it to them often enough. Being able to compliment your partner can help them to feel loved, valued, and aware of your feelings. Therefore, you won't take verbal marital communication skills with your partner lightly if you realize the value of communication in marriage. Such communication is essential for a lasting connection.

Nonverbal communication

We cannot understate the significance of communication in a marriage. We underestimate how much our body can communicate for us as humans. Be conscious of the messages your body language is sending to your spouse. When having unpleasant conversations with your spouse, face them and maintain an open body language. Your spouse will inadvertently detect a lack of vulnerability if you try to conduct an important talk while slumped over and walled off. No crossing of the legs. No arm-crossing. Your physical presence should communicate to your partner that you are willing to listen to what they have to say and to work through it. A closed-off posture is just one of several nonverbal indicators that communicate either negatively or positively.

Bodily Actions

preparing supper. visiting the supermarket removing the trash. going to get your pregnant wife some ice cream. These are all actions that you take to demonstrate to your spouse that you care about them rather than things you say. You can show your spouse how much you care about them by performing simple but considerate deeds. When discussing the value of communication in relationships, such physical gestures are especially helpful for couples who may not be particularly good at verbal communication. With this type of communication, the adage "actions speak louder than words" is relevant. Your body language should convey to your spouse that you are being truthful and open with them.

Husband and wife communication might act as a buffer against marital misunderstandings. Your partner is able to comprehend you better when you honestly discuss your thoughts, histories, desires, and beliefs.

Marriage communication gives you the chance to fully comprehend your spouse's thoughts and motivations, which can help you avoid misunderstandings. It guarantees that you won't be surprised by their subsequent acts, words, or ideas. Additionally, talking to your spouse during your marriage is the greatest way to sort up any misunderstandings you may have had with them. You may avoid any misunderstanding from hurting your relationship by communicating clearly and being upfront with one another.

FORGIVENESS

One of the hardest keys to adopt can be this one, especially if you tend to harbor grudges. Together with prayer and giving grace, this key is essential.

Both of those keys are extensions of forgiveness. Breathe deeply and ask your husband's pardon for forgetting to pause and get milk. Excuse your wife for reducing the size of your shirt.

It takes time and patience with both yourself and your partner to look at them and tell them that you forgive them for hurting you in the past, but forgiveness may improve your marriage.

However, if you are able to forgive your partner, you can move forward together without hostility or annoyance, and the hurt from the past can start to fade.

TRUST

Placing confidence and being able to depend on someone or something are the general definitions of trust. For close relationships, corporate organizations, society, and any individual to be somewhat happy, trust is important. Fear sets in when there is no trust. How then may trust be developed in a relationship?

A person's capacity to trust others can be influenced by a variety of life situations. The question of whether partners are faithful and honest enough with one another is at the heart of the trust issue in partnerships.

Being in a relationship depends most heavily on being able to trust your spouse. For a relationship to be satisfying, trust must be developed. A shattered relationship is one in which there is no trust or honesty.

Every relationship needs trust since it shows how much you can rely on the other person. Without trust, doubts and insecurities may rule the relationship. According to research, people value trust as a sign of loyalty as well as an indication of emotional closeness and vulnerability in a relationship. Without trust, your relationship might not be happy.

On trust, relationships are created. Trust demonstrates if you can rely on someone in a personal or professional capacity. You may see a life with your spouse and have a healthy connection once you can rely on them.

Some of the ways that we can build trust in our relationships include the following:

Clear Communication.

To increase trust in a relationship, partners should discuss their issues rather than keeping them to themselves and dwelling on them

Engage in face-to-face conversation wherever possible. The link between partners in a relationship is strengthened by direct and verbal communication. Please opt for more direct and personal communication rather than using emails or phone conversations. Make sure you maintain eye contact with your partner when speaking, as doing so helps to deepen the link between partners. These subtle nonverbal clues also assist partners in emphasizing the value of trust in a relationship.

Don’t conceal anything

If you think your relationship is plagued by secrets, how can you trust your partner? Transparency is essential for fostering trust in your relationship with your partner. If you’re learning to trust again, don’t compromise your integrity or keep secrets. Openness and honesty are necessary for building trust in relationships and marriages. Keeping secrets and developing trust in a relationship are incompatible goals. If you want to develop trust with your spouse, you must also make a plan to be honest and open with them. You must always be truthful in your interactions and communications with your partner if you want to be a reliable companion. How is trust established in a relationship? The straightforward solution to this is to avoid holding any secrets.

Say no more often.

If you feel confined by caving in to your partner’s demands, whether reasonable or outrageous, how can you trust in a relationship?

You are not required to agree to everything your partner asks for or suggests. It would be great if you weren’t made to suffer unpleasant experiences. Moving forward in a relationship built on equality will be simpler for both of you.

Remember to politely decline any requests they make if you don't like them in order to foster trust in your relationship. In any relationship, you shouldn't feel compelled to do something.

No deception

Do you ever wonder how to trust your boyfriend or girlfriend? Humans naturally have a propensity to find attraction in multiple people. However, this does not give you permission to cheat on your relationship.

The warning is that if you want to develop trust with your partner, you need keep the relationship exciting or else reevaluate your goals in life.

So how does one gain the trust of another person? Simply said, you shouldn't cheat on your partner because you no longer find them amusing or find enjoyment in their company.

In order to establish trust in a relationship, be sure to express your dissatisfaction with your partner's behavior.

Be attentive and involved.

Making the decision to be present with your partner is a relatively easy method to learn how to develop trust in a relationship.

Over time in relationships, complacency can creep in and cause you to emotionally distance yourself from your partner. Withholding from your mate might make insecurities worse and lead to relationship ambiguity.

You can reassure your spouse of your ongoing devotion to them and so contribute to the development of trust between you by being attentive to them and their needs

QUALITY TIME

Every couple has to spend quality time together for their relationship to advance and mature. But what occurs when one partner expresses their love through quality time? How does the desire for quality time especially when busy lives get in the way and affect the relationship?

Here's a closer look at how using the quality time love language might help your relationship and demonstrate to your "quality time" spouse that you are proficient in their preferred method of communication.quality time is the one that centers around togetherness. It's all about expressing your love and affection with your undivided attention.

When you're with your partner, you put down the cell phone, turn off the tablet, and focus on them. And, when you do that, it touches their heart in a way that really matters. They feel important, loved, and special like you were intentional in setting aside time just for them.

Unfortunately, thanks to technology, quality time with our partners is becoming more and more scarce. Even when we are together, we are someplace else—usually in cyberspace or deep in our own thoughts. But being in close proximity to one another while doing something else does not always constitute quality time, no matter how long you sit there. And for someone whose primary love language is quality time, this lack of connection can leave them feeling empty and alone.

How to Give Your Partner Quality Time

It's crucial to take actions that will make your mate feel loved and valued if you want to speak your partner's love language.

If spending quality time with your lover is their top love language, you should not only make time for them but also plan how you will spend it.

If you and your partner have different love languages, don't be shocked if at first these efforts feel a little forced. But with time and dedication, you'll find that you do these things for your mate without even thinking about it.

Here are a few ways you can express your love to your lover by spending quality time with them.

Use listening skills

One of the most loving things you can do for your partner is to actively listen to them, yet for many individuals, this doesn't come naturally. Instead, the majority of people give their own opinions and thoughts more thought than they do their partner's.

Try practicing the following active listening techniques when chatting with individuals you care about:

- Focus on what they are saying.
- Lean in slightly.
- Affirm what they are saying.
- Ask thoughtful questions.
- Avoid trying to offer advice, unless they ask for it.
- Try putting yourself in their shoes or thinking about how you might feel in the same situation.
- Quality time partners are more interested in feeling understood. They are looking for empathy and compassion and don't always want to have their situations fixed.

Set limit to technology

Nothing upsets a quality time person more than to communicate something they believe is incredibly important, only to look up and see their spouse is only partially paying listening while attempting to respond to a text or an email from a coworker.

Make it a habit to put your phone aside during meals or coffee breaks so that you can really listen to your companion. You may not talk about anything revolutionary, but by prioritizing your relationship with your partner over technology, you are showing essential and loving behavior.

Focus on Quality, Not Quantity

When it comes to spending quality time together, it's the caliber of your exchanges that matters more than how much time you spend together. And with so much going on in your life, finding a few minutes to have an in-depth chat with someone you love can be a great way to show them that you care.

The important thing is to make the effort to spend time with each other, even if it's only while you're chatting on the couch before heading to work. Keep in mind that quality time spent together is more important than quantity.

Make a Plan

While it's never a bad idea to be unplanned, especially with a special someone, planning an activity together may be just as thrilling and fun as a last-minute dinner or movie. After a while together, it's all too common for couples to fall into a rut.

Try establishing plans rather than accepting the "same old, same old." Making an effort to start quality time will be very important to your relationship. Additionally, the thought of spending time together will make them feel loved.

Whatever you decide to do, simply make a different plan. Below are a few ideas:

- Check out the newest eatery in town.

- Arrange a Saturday morning bike ride
- After work, arrange a leisurely stroll along the riverfront.

Develop a Routine

Find every day's little opportunities to connect with your companion. For instance, you may read the Sunday comics or pray or meditate together each morning. Finding a modest way to interact on a regular basis can make your partner feel satisfied and valued. Additionally, you might both anticipate doing it together.

Be present and available

Simply being present and spending time with your spouse through a trying moment can go a long way toward demonstrating your concern for them. Even while you won't be able to completely ease their suffering—and you shouldn't be expected to—you will be able to show that you are there for them and willing to help when they need it.

Stay in the moment

People that prioritize quality time as their primary form of communication never forget that time is finite and that tomorrow is not guaranteed. Because of this, they see quality time spent together as a gift that is both valuable and desirable in romantic relationships. They believe that living in the now is more important than doing anything else. It's also about putting your loved ones first above all else.

Get creative

There are days when everyone has a to-do list that is a mile long. Instead of doing everything by yourself, enlist the help of your special someone. You may squeeze in some quality time even while you are doing something uninteresting and routine.

For instance, stop listening to the radio and engage in conversation. Inquire about the state of your partner's life and what is worrying them right now. If you're inventive, you can use almost any activity as an opportunity to sneak in some quality time.

ACTS OF SERVICE

There's a fair possibility that acts of service are your love language if you feel most loved and cared for when your significant other takes on a duty so you have one less thing to worry about.

By observing how you express love to others, you can determine your love language as well. According to you may determine someone's love language by observing what they do for you. If you notice that your spouse frequently takes out the trash or refills your water glass when they realize it is empty, that may be their method of communicating to you that they value small acts of kindness from others and would like you to do the same for them.

Consider how your parents loved you when you were a child when determining whether acts of service are your love language. According to Sep, your love language frequently correlates to what your key attachment figures accomplished for you. You may have learn t to express love by acts of service, which later became your love language, if, for instance, your parents always had your favorite meal waiting for you in the morning or folded your laundry so you didn't have to.

What kind of deeds constitute acts of service?

According to experts, the following are a few examples of methods to demonstrate your love if acts of service are you or your significant other's love language:

- When their drink is empty, refill it.
- Allow them to sleep in so they can get a little additional rest while you get the kids ready for school or walk the dog.
- Make a lovely meal for them to eat or take them to a great restaurant at random so they won't have to cook when they get home.
- Help out around the house without being asked, whether it is with the dishes or other tasks.
- After a lengthy business trip, unpack their suitcase so they have one less thing to worry
- When they are ill, tend to their medical needs.
- When they're feeling tense or sore, offer to massage them.
- Perform chores for them.
- Plan the details of a trip so they don't have to.
- Arrange a party with their nearest and dearest to commemorate a birthday or other milestone.

Date night

Have a date night planned with your spouse

Dating is the suggestion that most couples miss and ignore when it comes to other advice for a happy marriage. What a couple does on their date night is irrelevant.

The link is strengthened and maintained throughout time by just spending time together one night a week. You should put your phones away and switch them off before going on a date so that you are not distracted.

Go rollerblading or trekking together, or watch a movie at home while eating popcorn. Be helpful and upbeat to one another, and switch things up frequently. A good marriage requires many steps, not just a romantic and thoughtful date night. If possible, arrange this for once a month.

SEX

A healthy marriage depends heavily on sexual intimacy. Therapists advise having sex on a regular basis, even if you're not feeling it .We advise chatting your preferences and adding any fantasy role-playing, poses, or bedroom props you may like to include to make the conversation fresh.

Good communication is essential for increasing both the amount AND quality of your sex. It's crucial to express your relationship's needs in general since effective communication fosters trust and sustains relationships. However, it is equally crucial to let your spouse know what you need in terms of sexual activity. Direct your spouse on how to do it correctly if they aren't doing it exactly as you want. Even though it could appear awkward or even like you might harm their feelings, ultimately they are just attempting to win your favor, so please assist them! And if your partner offers you instructions, thank them for their open and honest communication and follow their instructions. Intimacy is sometimes the first thing to disappear when life gets too overwhelming. When you have a lot going on and you are extremely stressed out, it can be difficult to think about sex or feel desirable. However, neglecting sex and intimacy during difficult times can seriously harm your relationship. Even if you think you don't have time for anything else in your day, it's crucial to have a close relationship with your partner. Making plans for private time with your partner might help to guarantee that your sexual needs are not neglected when things are hectic. When you're completely out of ideas, having a plan for sex can offer you something to look forward to.

Sexual intimacy is as important as romantic gestures. Talk about what turns you on, the positions or toys you'd like to try, your sexually sensitive spots, your secret fantasies and every other thing related to sex. This will both be exciting and revealing at the same time, and you'll find yourselves discovering new things about each other. However, this also includes problems in bed. Speak up about them or they will eventually turn around and bite you in the back. If your partner is not performing as expected or your sex drive has reduced drastically, talk about it. Think of or suggest new ways of handling it together and you will be one step towards overcoming these issues.

CONCLUSION

One's right to express their love and devotion to one another via marriage is a major event in one's life. It's a wonderful sensation to experience a close connection with someone who holds special meaning for you. A treasured aspect of life is having someone you can talk to and trusting them to have your best interests at heart. A person can experience unfathomable delight when they are in a relationship that is so intense and passionate. fostering a relationship when a couple has a life partner as well as a best friend that supports them through happy, sad, and occasionally nasty occasions. Marriage is a sacred relationship between two people that stands for the deepest levels of affection, trust, friendship, value, and lifetime commitment.

Finding the ideal partner involves a process, and after a series of interactions, a couple will decide whether or not they should date exclusively. A couple chooses to respect one other highly by taking that action, and they may even begin to fall in love as a result. The key is falling in love and learning to value not just the partner they have but also the qualities that person offers to their lives. The pair then has to learn that, sometimes, they must put the other person's feelings ahead of their own. Respect is essential in a relationship and can strengthen the connection.

In the process, maintaining the closest of friendships as a couple's marriage is essential to maintaining a joyful, positive connection. A marriage must have the ability to laugh together and enjoy one another. In order to keep things interesting and new, it is also a great idea to continue dating even after getting married. Having open lines of communication with one another is another crucial requirement for couple.

Your partner may sense your love by the way you treat them, how you feel about them, and how you weave your lives together. The sense of intimacy is also very significant because love is a feeling of connection and understanding. Your intimacy deepens as you share your aspirations, desires, and dreams with one another. I believe that the foundation of love is the closeness that true connection brings.

ABOUT THE AUTHOR

Paul Gottman is a writer, teacher and relationship consultant, whose work has healed so many broken relationships. his passion for writing gained him so many Global recognitions

www.ingramcontent.com/pod-product-compliance
Lightning Source LLC
LaVergne TN
LVHW020542160826
845677LV00015B/4157

* 9 7 9 8 8 4 7 2 4 9 3 0 0 *